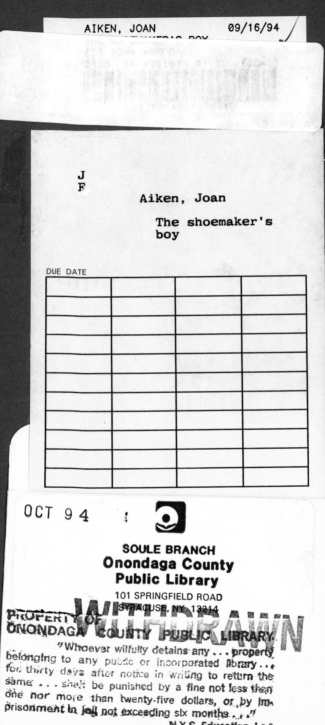

J
F

Aiken, Joan

The shoemaker's
boy

DUE DATE

THE SHOEMAKER'S BOY

JOAN AIKEN

THE SHOEMAKER'S BOY

ILLUSTRATED BY VICTOR G. AMBRUS

SIMON & SCHUSTER
BOOKS FOR YOUNG READERS

PUBLISHED BY SIMON & SCHUSTER
New York London Toronto Sydney Tokyo Singapore

SIMON & SCHUSTER BOOKS FOR YOUNG READERS
Simon & Schuster, Rockefeller Center
1230 Avenue of the Americas, New York, New York 10020
Text copyright © 1991 by Joan Aiken Enterprises Ltd.
Illustrations copyright © 1994 by Victor Ambrus
First published in Great Britain in 1991 by Simon & Schuster Young Books.
First U.S. edition 1994
All rights reserved including the right of reproduction
in whole or in part in any form.
SIMON & SCHUSTER BOOKS FOR YOUNG READERS
is a trademark of Simon & Schuster.
Designed by David Neuhaus.
The text of this book is set in Palatino.
Manufactured in the United States of America

10 9 8 7 6 5 4 3 2 1

Library of Congress Cataloging-in-Publication Data
Aiken, Joan.
The shoemaker's boy / by Joan Aiken ; illustrated by Victor Ambrus.
p. cm. Summary: When his father goes off on a long quest to find a way to
cure his wife's mysterious illness, a shoemaker's son has some strange and
frightening experiences. [1. Fairy tales. 2. Shoemakers—Fiction.]
I. Ambrus, Victor G., ill. II. Title.
PZ8.A266Sh 1994 [E]—dc20 93–6613 CIP
ISBN: 0–671–86647–8

CONTENTS

ONE

THREE STRANGE CHILDREN

Once there was a shoemaker's son called Jem. He lived with his parents in a small cottage and worked hard, learning his father's trade, making and mending all kinds of shoes.

But Jem was still young, not nearly so good at the craft as his father, when a worry came on the family. Jem's mother fell dreadfully ill, and no doctor seemed able to help her.

Day after day she lay asleep on her bed, white as bread, hardly breathing, unable to eat solid food. Jem and his father were afraid she would die. She never spoke, never stirred. Nothing would rouse her.

1

Jem's father decided to walk all the way to the Holy City of St. James in Spain, to pray that his wife might get better.

"If St. James can't help her, nobody can," he said. "You be a good boy now, Jem. Look after her as well as you can. And try to keep the customers satisfied."

Jem was worried about this plan, for his father was the best shoemaker in three kingdoms. People came from far away to have him measure their feet and make them boots or shoes. How would Jem ever manage on his own?

But he swallowed, and nodded, and waved a cheerful good-bye to his father, who stuck a scallop shell in his cap and walked away southward, along with a party of pilgrims who were on their journey to the Holy City of St. James, hundreds of miles away.

Weeks went by and months went by. Jem did his very best, making and mending shoes for the customers. Most of them were friendly and didn't ask too much, knowing about the family trouble. But, just the same, Jem longed for his father. Money grew short. He was falling further and further behind with his orders, for he could not work as quickly as his father, or do as much on his own as the two of them had done together. Half-finished pairs of shoes lay all over the cottage.

One evening Jem stepped outside for a quick breath of air after giving his mother her supper—milk with honey, which was all she would ever take, and no more of that than a spoonful—when he heard some faint, shrill, twittering voices behind him, and turned around to see three strange little children.

Were they children? They had wizened little faces and thin, sticklike little arms and legs, and they came up no higher than his waist. They were all dressed in green.

"What did you say?" Jem asked, looking at them in surprise, for he had never seen anything like them before. Where in the world could they have come from?

"If you please, master, we have come for the three silver keys."

"Keys? What keys?" said Jem. "I have no silver keys."

"But, if you please, master, we were sent to ask you for them. The three silver keys. They were to be left with you. And we were to get them."

Jem shook his head, even more puzzled. "No one said anything to me about three silver keys. You must be wrong. And where in the name of goodness did you come from, you strange little things?"

But when Jem said "in the name of goodness," the three rickety little creatures disappeared, vanished clean away— *phttt!*—just like that!

Jem rubbed his eyes, and rubbed them again.

"I must have dreamed them," he said to himself. "I'm tired, very tired—that's all."

He had good reason to be tired. For, night after night these last weeks, he had sat up, watching over his mother, feeding her a spoonful of milk every hour.

TWO

THE BLACK KNIGHT

That night he worked late and was about to lie down on the cobbler's bench for half an hour's rest, when there came a loud *bang* on the door.

Bother! Maybe it's those three children back again, thought Jem, not at all pleased at being disturbed. He was in no hurry to answer.

But the knock came again—*thump, thump!*—very sharp and impatient. It sounded too strong and rough to be the children. So Jem sighed, rubbed his eyes and his face, crossed the room, and unbarred the door.

Outside stood a knight. In the dusky light, Jem could just see that he was dressed all in black—over his armor he wore a black tunic, and his shield and helmet were of black metal, his cloak was black, and so was the great horse that stood behind him, steaming and stamping and shaking its head.

"Hey, boy! I want you to make me a pair of boots," said the knight. "I have heard that the footwear you make here is the best in the land."

"Oh, sir, I'm afraid my father is away from home," said Jem. "I may not be able to make them as well as your honor wishes."

"You look to me like a clever boy, as well as a truthful one," said the knight. "I'll take a chance, for I have traveled a great distance to come here."

Indeed, when the knight walked inside

and Jem had lit a candle, he could guess that this must be so; the knight's cloak and tunic were worn and dusty, and the boots he wore were split and cracked.

Jem knelt to measure the knight's feet. He was too polite to exclaim, but the shape of them surprised him greatly. He had never seen such feet before in his whole life. And, by now, Jem had measured a great many feet.

"What is your price for a pair of boots?" said the knight.

"One guinea, sir."

"I will give you two. But the boots must be finished by breakfast time."

Jem thought that if he worked all night he could just about manage this. And two guineas would buy enough milk and honey to last his mother for weeks, besides leather and firewood and candles and thread and shoemakers' needles.

"I will do my best to have them ready for you, sir," said Jem, hurriedly reaching for his shears to begin cutting the leather.

"The boots must be black. Oh, and by the way," said the knight, very carelessly, as he turned to leave, "I think three silver keys have been left here for me? You may as well give them to me now."

Outside the door the knight's black horse let out a shrill neigh. The sound was so loud and sudden that it brought Jem's skin out in goosepimples.

"No, sir," he said. "I'm afraid you are wrong. Nobody has left any keys with me."

"No? Perhaps they will have before I come for the boots. Keep them for me carefully."

And the knight strode out. He did not say good-bye. And Jem felt a great deal more comfortable when he had gone and the sound of his horse's hooves had died away.

ThREE

THE WHITE KNIGHT

That night, Jem worked harder than he had ever before in his life, cutting and snipping, stitching and stretching and shaping. One candle burned clean away, and he had to light another. Still, never mind, the black knight's money would pay for plenty of candles.

One boot was finished, and the other well begun, when he heard another knock at the door.

Oh, plague take whoever it is, thought Jem. It can't be the black knight back yet, for it's not long past midnight, nowhere near breakfast time. Maybe it is those green children again, botheration befall them!

He called out, "Please go away, whoever you are! I'm very busy."

But a soft voice answered, "I promise I will take no more than a moment of your time."

Something about the voice made Jem think of his father. It certainly did not belong to those strange little children. So, rather impatiently, he unbarred the door again and looked out.

The moon was up now and by its light he could see a knight standing on the path. His cloak and tunic were white, his armor was of silver, so were his sword and the helmet that hung on his shoulders. On his shield Jem could see a crest showing three keys.

"Good evening, Jem," he said. "I am sorry to disturb you at your work, but I have heard that you are a good and trustworthy boy. I have come to ask a favor of you. You see this little packet? I need to leave it in a safe place while I go on an errand. May I leave it with you? And will you make sure that nobody, nobody at all, takes it or touches it?"

The knight handed Jem a small square of folded white silk, about the size of a purse, tied across and across with dozens of threads.

"Why, certainly, sir," said Jem, puzzled but polite. "I'll keep it carefully for you, if you wish. It shall go up here, on my top shelf. And I will see that no one touches it. But when will you be back for it?"

"If I am not back by daybreak," said the knight, "you may keep the packet. Good night to you now." And he sprang onto his white horse, which bolted away with the speed and silence of lightning.

Jem put the packet on the shelf, relocked the door, and went back to work.

Now he was very tired indeed and found it harder and harder to set his stitches. His head nodded, and, what was worse, he thought he kept hearing voices. He heard the voices of the green, shriveled children, wailing and squeaking outside the door.

"Let us in, Jem! Let us in to sit by your fire! We are perishing with cold, Jem. We are hungry and freezing. We need those three keys, we need them dreadfully. Let us in, please, please, let us in and give us the keys!"

"I have no keys for you!" Jem shouted, waking himself out of his dream, and he set to work again harder than ever.

Then he thought he heard the black knight, riding round and round outside the cottage, and he heard the black horse stamp and snort and whinny.

"You had better give me those keys, Jem," shouted the black knight.

"I can't do that, sir. I promised that no one would touch them."

"Fool boy! Those keys were left for me!"

Jem shook himself and trembled as he thought he heard the horse whinny again. And then he heard what sounded like a wild battle: there were thumps and clangs and bangs, shouts and blows and screams, the neighing of several horses and the trample of many hooves.

Whatever is going on out there is no business of mine, thought Jem. My business is to get this boot finished. And he ducked his head over his work, stitching and stitching away for dear life.

Once or twice he went to see how his mother was, in the back room, wondering that she was not roused by the sounds outside. But no, she lay as before, in her deep, strange sleep.

FOUR

THE SILK PACKET

Just before daybreak the second boot was done. They are by far the best boots I have ever made, thought Jem, looking at them with pride as they stood side by side on the bench, soft and supple, finely stitched and gleaming with polish.

Now there came a crashing thump on the door. The bolt broke and the door swung open. There stood the black knight, looking blacker than ever against the slowly growing light of day. He was all dusty and bleeding, his armor hacked and gashed. His shield was scratched and dented, and so was his helmet, through the bars of which his eyes gleamed angrily.

23

It was plain that he had been in a fight, and, from the way he looked, he had got the worst of it.

"I've come for my boots, boy," he snapped. "Are they ready?"

"Yes, sir, quite ready," said Jem, and pointed to them, standing on the bench.

The knight tossed two gold coins on the floor. He said, "And I'll have those keys, too."

"I have no keys for you, sir."

"Don't lie to me! The white knight left three keys for me in a silk packet. There they are—on the shelf. It was for me he left them!"

The knight stepped forward to snatch the packet from the shelf, but Jem was there before him. He whipped them away and sprang to the back of the shop, where he stood holding the little silk square with its crisscross of thread.

"Give it to me!" growled the knight through the bars of his helmet. "Take off that cursed wrapping and give it to me! Or I will slice your head clean off."

"No, sir. I have no right to give it to you."

The black knight moved forward a step, pulling his sword from the scabbard— and, just at that moment, the old rooster, perched on the roof above, crowed *cockadoodledoo*!

Jem saw the pair of black boots he had
made wither and shrivel away like paper
burning in a blaze. Looking above the
boots he saw that the black knight, too,
had vanished clean away. And so had the
gold coins.

Nothing was left but the little white
packet that he held in his hand.

Well, thought Jem, the white knight did
say that if he was not back by daybreak, I

might keep the packet. And the sun has risen. So I may as well open it and see what is inside.

Very carefully he snipped through all the threads that tied the packet, across and across. Then he undid the white silk wrapping. He had expected to find three silver keys, but no—he found only a little square of thin, soft, white bread. Quite fresh it seemed, considering that it had been wrapped and tied up so tight for who knows how long.

"Jem!"came his mother's voice faintly through the door. "Jem? I'm hungry, Jem!"

Jem was thunderstruck, for it had been months since his mother had spoken.

"*Mother!* Are you feeling better?"

"I'm so hungry," she said, faintly stirring. "Oh, how I would like to eat a little piece of fresh white bread. . . ."

FIVE

A PRAYER
IS ANSWERED

Two months later, Jem's father came home—thin, worn, weary, footsore, gray-haired, with his clothes frayed and torn and tattered. But, my goodness! How happy he was to see his wife strong and active and pink-cheeked again and to find how well his boy, Jem, had managed, making and mending shoes and boots, keeping the customers satisfied during the long months of his absence.

29

And, when they asked him—"Yes!" he said. "I got to the Holy City of St. James. What a place! A main square the size of a town, and a church the size of a whole forest. I begged and prayed the saint to help us—and see how quickly he answered my prayer!

"But there was one moment, on the way, when I thought I should never reach the city or see either of you again. For a band of brigands, led by a wicked fellow in black armor, attacked our party in wild mountain country; and they would have killed us all if we had not been rescued at the very last minute."

"Who rescued you, father?"

"A knight, all dressed in white. He was the best fighter I've ever seen—finished off half a dozen of the robbers, and the rest turned around and ran for their lives.

"The knight wouldn't even stay to be thanked—said he had another errand, a long way off; and he galloped away before we could even find out his name. But the crest on his shield showed three keys."

ABOUT THE AUTHOR

Joan Aiken was born in Rye, England, and her first poem was published when she was only sixteen. Her father is the American poet Conrad Aiken, and her sister, Jane Aiken Hodge, is a novelist.

Joan Aiken is the author of some sixty books for adults and young people, including *The Wolves of Willoughby Chase*. Her writings also include verse, plays, short stories, and nonfiction. She lives in Petworth, England, with her husband, an American painter.

ABOUT THE ARTIST

Victor G. Ambrus was born in Budapest and attended the Hungarian Academy of Fine Arts and the Royal College of Art, London. He is the author and illustrator of a dozen books for young readers, and has illustrated more than two hundred books. He has received two Greenaway Gold Medals for illustration.

Mr. Ambrus lives in Surrey, England.